The Wonder Series

W9-CHV-509

# Wild Horses

Stories and Activities

by

— • —

CAROL ANN MOORHEAD

— • —

Illustrations

by

Kay Herndon

and

Gail Kohler Opsahl

## Denver Museum
## of Natural History

## WILD HORSES

Supported by Wild Horse and Burro National Program Office, Bureau of Land Management. For more information on wild horses, write to:

Bureau of Land Management
Dept. DM
P.O. Box 12000
Reno, Nevada 89520

Published in the United States of America by
Roberts Rinehart Publishers
Post Office Box 666
Niwot, Colorado 80544

Published in Great Britain, Ireland, and Europe by
Roberts Rinehart Publishers
Main Street, Schull, West Cork
Republic of Ireland

Distributed in the United States and Canada by
Publishers Group West

Library of Congress Catalog Card Number
94-74046

International Standard Book Number
1-879373-51-3

Manufactured in the United States of America

Trading card photography by
George McDonald ©1994, Denver, CO

Navajo song, page 30, reprinted from *The Navajo Indians,*
Dane and Mary Roberts Coolidge, Houghton-Mifflin Co.,
New York, 1930. Quote on page 48–49, reprinted with
permission of Macmillan Books for Young Readers, an
imprint of Simon & Schuster, from *Mustang: Wild Spirit
of the West,* by Marguerite Henry, ©1966 Macmillan
Publishing Company.

## AUTHOR'S ACKNOWLEDGMENTS

A wonderful band of professionals helped make *Wild Horses* possible. Core members of the band were Betsy Armstrong, Kay Herndon, and Gail Kohler Opsahl of the Denver Museum of Natural History, and Kris Eshelman of the U.S. Bureau of Land Management. I thank them for their humor and support. I am especially grateful to Gail for enhancing the activities with her creative ideas and "engineering" skills. I thank the book's editor, Karen Nein, and DMNH reviewers: Polly Andrews, Diana Lee Crew, Joyce Herold, Dr. Cheri Jones, and Dr. Richard Stucky. A special note of thanks to Jamie Alton of DMNH, who compiled the glossary and researched last-minute facts, and to Tina McDonald of the BLM, who helped gather facts for the wild horse trading cards.

I am particularly indebted to Dawn Lappin for her wisdom and knowledge about wild horses, and to Tom Pogacnik of the BLM for an informative tour in Nevada's wild horse country. I am also grateful to my niece, Marissa, and my neighbor, Mia, for commenting on parts of the manuscript, and to the students of St. Anne's School, who tested the activities. A special thanks also to my mother-in-law, Jean, for her review of the story, and to my husband, Luke, for developing a keen interest in wild horses.

—*Carol Ann Moorhead*

# Contents

# Introduction

When I was young, I daydreamed a lot. I remember dreaming of wild horses. They were short and scruffy, and their tails whipped in the wind. Sometimes they stood sleepily amid tufts of pale green grass. Other times, they ran—and I ran, too, but I couldn't catch them. They disappeared before my mind's eye every time.

I don't remember wanting to become a horse. I just wanted to join that daydream herd. I wanted to whinny and snort, kick up my heels, and feel the wind blowing through my own tangled mane. Most of all, I wanted to feel free and on my own. I think it was the wildness of those horses that interested me most.

Since beginning this book, I've noticed that wild horses interest many people. Some are the daydreamers; they sigh or smile when I mention wild horses. Others are more scientific; they've read about wild horses and want to know which ones I'm writing about.

## WILD OR FERAL?

Believe it or not, "Which ones?" is a tricky question to answer. There are two kinds of wild horses—horses that are truly wild and those that live in a wild condition. This book discusses both.

Truly wild horses have never been **domesticated**, or tamed by humans. An example is the Przewalski's horse of Asia, the probable ancestor of today's domestic horse.

Horses that live in a wild condition roam free today, but their ancestors—or they themselves—were once domesticated. Biologists refer to these horses as **feral** animals. The wild horses of the American West are feral, as are the horses of Assateague Island off the coast of Virginia and Maryland.

This book is about all free-roaming horses, but it pays particular attention to the wild horses of the American West, commonly called **mustangs**. Although feral by definition, U.S. law recognizes mustangs as wild animals. Whether feral or legally wild, these horses are *wild* in spirit—hence the name of the book: *Wild Horses*.

# The Black Foal

As the plane descended into Reno, Nevada, Sara pressed her face up against the window. Below were steep ridges and valleys among softer, more rounded mountains. Sara strained her eyes and searched the hillsides. She couldn't see them, but in her head she could hear them—their hooves hitting hard-packed dirt, a snort, a squeal—the wild ones, the mustangs, the bands of wild horses she'd read about.

The plane touched down with a jolt and taxied up to the gate. Sara exited, and before she knew it, was nearly squeezed in half by her aunt Ronnie, who was laughing and bursting with energy, just as Sara remembered her.

"Let's go see some wild horses!"

"Right now?!" Sara asked.

"Yep, they rounded up a hundred or so off the range, and today's the first day they're up for adoption. I volunteered to help out and plumb forgot to cancel when your dad told me you were coming."

"That's okay," Sara said agreeably, but the truth was she was disappointed. She hadn't pictured seeing her first wild horses behind fences.

At the fairgrounds Sara jumped out of the pickup truck amid corrals of shaggy horses. Her eyes leapt from back to back: roan, paint, buckskin, bay.

"Look at them all!" she whispered.

"Yeah, quite a sight," her aunt said, coming up from behind. "Come on, let's have a look around!"

"They're not exactly show horses," she said as they approached the first corral. "At least not yet."

Sara had to agree. They were far from being show horses, but they weren't wild either. They weren't pawing the ground, or flaring their nostrils, or standing tall and alert. Instead they were huddled together, swishing their tails, looking like any group of penned-up horses. Sara's heart sank.

"They use helicopters to round up the horse bands out on the . . ."

"Helicopters!?" Sara exclaimed, "I thought cowboys rounded them up."

"Cowboys, or 'wranglers,' as horse people like to be called . . . They still round 'em up in canyon country, but nowadays it's the chopper pilots who do most of the wrangling."

Sara had heard about all she cared to hear. She eyed the latch on the corral gate next to her. She imagined opening it, whooping and shooing the horses to freedom. She saw them running, their tails flying. Then her dream stopped— Aunt Ronnie put her hand on her shoulder.

"Go on down there," she said, pointing to a crowd at the far end of the fairgounds. "You'll enjoy it. I'll be at the BLM office if you need me." She walked toward a small trailer with "Bureau of Land Management" painted on its side.

Sara looked back at the crowd and suddenly felt shy and self-conscious. She remembered what her dad told her at the airport. Aunt Ronnie will look after you, he'd said, but she'll expect you to be independent-minded. Sara turned and headed toward the crowd. Shorts, sandals, and all, she joined cowboys and cowgirls alongside the corral.

Inside a man and a horse were intently focused on each other's movements. "It's all about establishing trust," the man said in a soft, easy voice. He stepped forward, propelling the horse into a nervous trot.

Sara overheard the boy beside her whispering, "These gentling techniques calm 'em down, but they don't break their spirit."

One look at his dusty silver spurs and Sara figured he knew what he was talking about. Casually, she sidestepped toward him.

"You just watch," the boy continued, "he'll be on this horse's back in two hours."

"Really?" Sara heard herself saying, her face flushing red as she spoke.

But the silver-spurred boy didn't seem to mind at all that she'd been eavesdropping. He just turned and smiled at her.

"Hard to believe, isn't it?" he said. And darn if he wasn't right. In an hour the horse was following the man around the corral like a puppy dog. In two hours, the man was lying across his back like a sack of flour. Sara stood by the silver-spurred boy and watched it all happen.

When she turned to leave, he asked, "Are you Maggie Lando?"

"N-no," Sara said, noticing how shiny black his hair was.

"Oh, sorry, I thought you might be," he stammered. "She's a barrel racer. Someone told me she had strawberry hair," he said, glancing up at her head, then stuffing his hands into pockets on either side of the biggest silver buckle Sara had ever seen.

"I don't know much about barrel racing," Sara admitted.

"You're not from around here, are you?"

"I'm from Virginia," she said, suddenly aware of her accent.

"Never been there," the boy replied, followed by a mile-long pause.

"My name's Sara," she said, extending her hand, like she'd been taught to do in the company of strangers. The boy grabbed her hand and shook it firmly.

"Mine's Sam, Sam Reed."

Right then the man in the corral walked up, only now he was on the outside. Sam introduced Sara to his father, the horse trainer. He was quiet and gentle, Sara thought, just like he was with the horse. As soon as she spoke, Mr. Reed made the connection to her aunt. "With an accent like that you must be Ronnie Carter's niece from Virginia," he said with a warm smile. "She told me you were coming." Sara was glad that he and Aunt Ronnie were friends, and that he was training one of her horses. Maybe it meant she and Sam could go riding together.

— • —

Aunt Ronnie's horse ranch was on the outskirts of Reno. As soon as they arrived Sara could see that Aunt Ronnie wasn't going to make any special holes in her schedule. She was too busy running the ranch. This suited Sara just fine as long as she could help groom and exercise the horses. It suited her even better when she heard Mr. Reed would be out with his son the next few days.

The next morning while Aunt Ronnie and Mr. Reed worked with her new Arabian, Sara and Sam headed out on horseback.

"I've been wanting to show my dad something out here for a long time," Sam said as they passed through a gate marked "Entering Public Lands." "You might be the first person I show it to."

"Show what to?"

"You'll know it if we see it," he replied, "at least I think you will."

Sara took that for a challenge and kept her eyes out for something unusual. Problem was almost everything looked different to her: the wide-open sky, the sea green sagebrush, just the simple fact that she could see so far. Sara stretched her eyes to the horizon. Something caught her eye. It looked like a dust devil, or smoke maybe.

"Sam, you see something out there?" she asked, holding her eyes on the growing cloud. If Sam answered, she never heard him. Sara stared the dust cloud down, but stares and all, it disappeared. "It's gone!" she shouted. "It was right there, and now it's gone."

"It's just the land playing tricks," Sam said. "Keep watching."

Sara fixed her eyes on the spot where she saw the cloud disappear, just the other side of a yellow blooming rabbitbrush. The air was warming up and the saddle leather creaked beneath her as her aunt's horse shifted from hoof to hoof. Sara leaned forward to rub his neck. "It's okay Cactus, we'll get movin—"

She heard it before she saw it. Her head shot up just as Sam shouted "Over there! That's it, that's them!"

Topping a rise only a couple hundred yards away was a streaming band of horses. They ran head to flying tail across the ridgeline.

"Get off!" Sam said, sliding off his horse. Sara swung her leg over, keeping an eye on the mustangs as they cut a jagged path down through sage and bitterbrush. Her heart was racing. Sam led Smokestack to the bottom of the knoll. Sara followed with Cactus. "Quick, weight down your reins," Sam said, rolling a rock onto the loose ends of Smokestack's reins.

Like a pair of sidewinders, Sam and Sara slithered on their bellies to an outcropping of rocks. Not far below was a long draw divided by a small stream and dotted with trees. They were just in time. A speckled foal galloped into view. Sara gasped. Right behind was a dappled grey.

"That's mom," Sam whispered. And then one, two, three palomino mares, each with a sure-footed foal.

Sara was busy making vows to never, ever adopt a wild horse. Out here is the only place they belong, she was thinking, when a buckskin stallion as wild as a hawk's cry entered the draw.

"There he is!" Sam whispered. Sara wriggled up higher on the rock.

The stallion was trotting, his black mane rising like smoke off white embers. He tossed his head and rolled his fiery eyes as he circled his harem. Suddenly he stopped and wheeled around. A coal black foal, all legs and air, ran into view. The stallion flattened his ears, and charged. The frightened foal leapt to the side, shook its dainty head, and trotted toward the mares.

As the foal approached, one of the palominos squealed and kicked. Another charged at him, and the third laid back her ears and flashed her teeth. "He must belong to the grey," Sara whispered, as the foal stepped toward the dappled mare.

"Twins are rare," Sam responded. As soon as he spoke, the dappled grey lowered its neck and drove the black foal away.

Tears sprung into Sara's eyes. "Why won't she take him?" she asked. The black foal stood splay-legged and bewildered at the edge of the harem.

"She has her own foal, they all do," he answered. "Something must have happened to his mother."

"You think she's dead?" Sara asked.

"I'd guess so," Sam replied. "Look how skinny he is."

They watched as the mares pulled at sparse bunchgrasses and ate sprigs of saltbush, their own foals huddled at their sides, suckling milk.

"Yeah, there's barely enough grass and shrubs for them to support one foal," Sam whispered. "It was a bad year for rain and what little grew has gotta be shared by cows, deer, and mustangs. There's not much to go around."

Sara looked at the dry, rocky ground. "If he doesn't get milk, he's going to die," she said matter-of-factly, wiping the tears from her eyes. "How long will they stay here, do you think?"

"Not long, they'll drink awhile, then move on," Sam replied.

Sara inched back down the rock outcrop, and sat upright. "Then we have to move fast," she said.

"But we don't have time to get the BLM out here," Sam said.

"Precisely," Sara responded. "That's why we have to do it ourselves."

"Do what?"

"Round him up," she said. "You can rope a steer, can't you?"

"Yes," said Sam, his eyes widening as he realized what Sara was saying. Quickly she laid out her plan. Before Sam could argue, Sara was on Cactus, heading down a gully to the entrance of the draw.

Sam hopped on Smokestack and headed uphill to a point where he could cross the ridgeline and drop into the draw. Hidden by a string of trees, Sam eased in behind a clump of junipers. He uncoiled his rope, and tossed it out to remove the kinks. Then he pulled it up, coil by coil, and made a loop big enough to slip over the little foal's head.

Meanwhile, Sara waited at the mouth of a gully that opened into the draw. Heart racing, she watched the mares and foals climb out of the streambed, leaving the stallion behind. If the mares took off now, the black foal would follow before the stallion. Sara knew the danger of coming up against him. He'd surely think Cactus was trying to steal his mares. Sara glanced up the draw and prayed Sam was ready.

The lead mare started down the draw. The black foal perked its ears. Sara gripped her reins and glanced toward the streambed. The first palomino and the second followed. Then the third. The foal trotted forward a few feet. Sara's legs tightened around Cactus.

Suddenly the stallion leapt out of the streambed, bluffed a charge at the orphaned foal, and raced after the others. The foal stood still a moment, then took off from behind.

Timing was everything now. Sara leaned forward, and dropped her hands low on Cactus's neck. As soon as the stallion raced past, Cactus bolted into the draw. The frightened foal planted his hind feet, slid to a dusty stop, turned, and ran flat out for a gully on the other side. Sara pulled up, and watched Sam take over.

Sam and Smokestack were flying down the draw, Sam's rope singing in wide arcing loops above his head. The foal was closing in on the gully.

"Now Sam, now!" Sara whispered.

As if he'd heard, Sam rose up and snapped his wrist. The loop sailed out ahead, ahead of Smokestack, ahead of the foal, and then dropped—Sara couldn't believe it—right over the foal's head.

"You did it!" Sara shouted as she rode up.

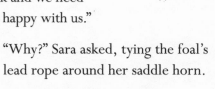

"We did it—good work cutting him off at the pass!" Sam said, jumping off Smokestack. "He's skinny, but he's a beauty!"

Sara slid down off Cactus and held her hand out to the foal. He tossed his head and struggled against the end of the rope.

"He's as wild as his father," she said. "I wish he could stay that way."

"Least he won't starve to death," Sam said. "Come on, let's get him back to your aunt's. He needs some milk and we need to call the BLM. They're not going to be too happy with us."

"Why?" Sara asked, tying the foal's lead rope around her saddle horn.

"Only the BLM is supposed to round up horses out here," Sam replied.

The sun was high in the sky now, and hot. Sam and Sara rode in silence until heavy wingbeats stirred the air. "Ravens," Sam said. Sara watched two large birds fly overhead, their black feathers shining in the high sun.

"How about 'Raven' for a name?" Sara asked. Sam didn't answer. He was busy watching a vehicle in the distance.

"Sara, that's a BLM truck. I'm going to try to catch it before it leaves." Smokestack kicked up a plume of dust as they galloped off. Sara kept moving, whispering words of encouragement to Raven as he trailed behind. Before long, Sam was back, wearing a bright smile.

"We are lucky today!" he said, catching his breath. "Only reason you and I aren't in a heap of trouble is 'cause that BLM biologist spotted our band a few days ago. And yesterday she found the dead mare."

"Does that mean we can keep him?" Sara asked.

"No, she'll swing by the ranch with a trailer at the end of the week to pick him up. He'll go up for adoption after that."

Sara knew it had to be, but she was sad anyway.

— • —

The Carson City wild horse adoption began the next weekend. Sam and Sara had agreed to meet.

Aunt Ronnie was volunteering at the BLM table where people were dropping names in a hat. The adoption would get under way when they started pulling the names back out. Meanwhile folks were milling around with clipboards, writing down the numbers of their favorite horses. Sara searched the corrals and found Raven with other long-legged foals. "Number 67," she read on his tag.

"Hey, Number 67," she said, tears welling up in her eyes.

Raven looked up. "Come here, Raven," Sara whispered, not sure if he would recognize her. "No bottles of milk today, but at least I can pet you." Raven stepped forward and pressed his muzzle against Sara's fingers.

"That one will do," Sara heard a man behind her saying. "Write down 67, son!" Sara looked up as a gruff-looking man spat a stream of tobacco juice at her feet. He winked at Sara, spat again, and walked away with his son.

"What does he mean—'that one'll do'?" Sara grumbled. She kneeled down and leaned her forehead against the fence. "Don't worry, Raven," she said, stroking his muzzle. "I'm sure his name's at the bottom of the hat." But Sara wasn't sure of anything; she was scared.

Just then a microphone crackled and a man's voice boomed over the fairgrounds. The adoption was about to begin. Sara stood up as the BLM man pulled a slip of paper out of the hat. Slowly he unfolded it.

"The pick of the herd goes to Mr. Roger Bronn," he announced. Sara's eyes raced around to find the tobacco-spitting man. There he was, over by the burro pen. The real Mr. Bronn stepped up to the BLM table, a little girl holding his hand. Sara breathed deeply.

Right then Sam walked up. "Anyone showing interest in Raven yet?" he asked, lightly tapping her new hat. "Nice ha—" he started to say when a young boy excused himself and stepped between Sam and Sara.

"Here's a black one, Mom! Number 67." he said, pointing to Raven. "He's pretty, isn't he?" The boy looked at his mom with eyes that sparkled. She smiled and nodded back at him.

"If you're looking for a pretty black horse," Sara heard Sam say, "there's one that's not quite so skinny two corrals down." The mother thanked Sam and guided the boy in the direction he'd pointed.

"Why did you do that? He would have been perfect for Raven!" Sara exclaimed.

"I have a hunch there's someone better," he said. Sara spun on the heel of her boot, and knelt down beside Raven. The microphone crackled again. She dropped her head against the fence post to hide her rising tears.

"The next person to choose a horse today," the announcer said, "is Ms. Ronnie Carter!" Sara jerked her head around to the BLM table where Aunt Ronnie was jumping to her feet. Wide-eyed and smiling, she whispered something to the announcer.

"Number 67!" his voice boomed. "As soon as this little foal is off milk and eating hay, he's headed to Virginia!"

Aunt Ronnie smiled, Sam winked, and Raven's breath was warm and damp on Sara's fingers.

*The End*

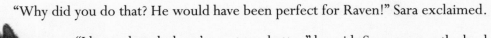

## KEY TO FREEZE MARK SYMBOLS

Each wild horse in the Adopt-A-Horse Program receives a unique mark on its neck. Instead of using hot branding irons to mark the horses, the BLM uses less painful cold irons. Each iron is frozen in -346°F (-210°C) liquid nitrogen. A veterinarian or trained assistant places the frosty iron against the horse's neck just long enough to turn the hair white.

A U.S. government symbol
Year of birth from top to bottom
State registration number

BLM    81    0    3    1    9    8    7

# Adopt-A-Horse Program

Raven is just one of hundreds of thousands of wild horses that have been gathered from U.S. public lands and adopted by people like Sara and you.* With the help of wild horse supporters, the U.S. Bureau of Land Management (BLM) started the Adopt-A-Horse or Burro Program in 1973. By reducing the number of wild horses living on the range, as well as cattle and sheep, the BLM hopes to improve **habitat** for all animals. Habitat is the place where an animal or a plant normally lives.

Each year the BLM rounds up horses in areas where too many grazing animals threaten the habitat. They are taken to wild horse centers where they receive veterinary care, a freeze mark, and plenty of food and water. From there the horses are moved to adoption sites—often fairgrounds—all over the country. Adoptions are good places to see wild horses up close.

Taming a wild horse is easier than it sounds. Unlike the old "breaking" techniques, today's methods work with the horse's instincts. The new process, called "gentling," is kinder to the horse, and safer for both horse and trainer. With proper training, most wild horses can be ridden within months. Many become excellent—even famous—pleasure, show, or work horses. See the wild horse trading cards included in this book for examples.

## OBJECTIVE
◆ To decipher freeze mark symbols.

## YOU NEED
◆ A pencil
◆ The "Key to Freeze Mark Symbols" on page 16 and the list of state freeze mark numbers on this page.

## TO DO
1. Look for freeze marks on the necks of horses on page 5. (Hint: there are three visible freeze marks.)
2. Using the key on page 16, decipher the symbols to identify the three freeze mark numbers. Write them on the lines provided.
3. After you find out the birth year of each, check the six-digit registration numbers against the state list to learn in which state each horse was gathered.

### Bureau of Land Management
# FREEZE MARK NUMBERS
—✳—

| | |
|---|---|
| 000000 to 080000 | Oregon |
| 080001 to 160000 | Arizona |
| 160001 to 240000 | California |
| 240001 to 320000 | Colorado |
| 320001 to 400000 | Idaho |
| 400001 to 480000 | Montana |
| 480001 to 640000 | Nevada |
| 640001 to 720000 | New Mexico |
| 720001 to 800000 | Utah |
| 800001 to 880000 | Wyoming |
| 880001 to 880100 | Eastern States |

*According to U.S. law, you must be 18 years or older to adopt a horse. But it is common for parents or legal guardians, who meet certain other requirements, to adopt one for a child.

# Wild Horses of the World

Wild horses live throughout the world. They live in the grasslands and deserts of North America, Africa, Asia, Australia, and Europe.

All horses have the same general shape, but their colors, patterns, and sizes may surprise you. Take zebras for instance. Did you know they are wild horses with stripes? And don't be fooled by the long ears of wild asses . . . they are horses, too.

In fact, there are seven **species**, or types, of horses, six of which are truly wild. An eighth went extinct in recent history. Scientists group these closely related species together in a general category—the **genus** *Equus.* The species you are most familiar with is *Equus caballus,* the everyday horse of farms, rodeos, and riding rings.

*Equus caballus*, or *E. caballus* for short, is the only species for which there are no truly wild horses left. Members of the species are either domesticated or feral. The wild herds of *E. caballus* that roam free in parts of North and South America, Australia, Europe, and Asia are feral descendants of released or runaway domestic horses.

## OBJECTIVE

◆ Create a world map of wild horse species and discover their habitats and survival status.

## THIS ACTIVITY INCLUDES

◆ "Wild Horses of the World Map," pages 22 and 23
◆ "Wild Horses of the World Cards," page 19

## YOU NEED

◆ Scissors
◆ Glue, paste, or tape

## TO ASSEMBLE

1. Cut along the dashed lines on pages 21 and 24. Cut on three sides only, like doors.
2. Cut out the "Wild Horse Cards" on page 19.
3. Fold each card along the solid line so that the picture covers up the type.
4. Match the letters on the tabs of the "Wild Horse Cards" to the letters on pages 21 and 24. Paste the "Wild Horse Cards" by the shaded lettered tabs only, picture side down.
5. After all cards are pasted into place, turn to the map on pages 22 and 23. Open the doors to disclose which horse species live where. Read the horse's name, see its picture, and open the picture to read all about it.

# WILD HORSES OF THE WORLD CARDS

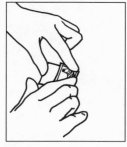

Fold card to cover type

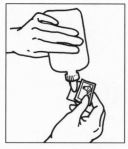

Paste shaded tab only

Match letters and paste down

Open doors on map to read

A A
Paste
A A
Paste
A A

### *Equus zebra*

STATUS: Of the two subspecies of mountain zebra, one is Endangered and the other is Threatened.

---

B B
Paste
B B
Paste
B B

### *Equus grevyi*

STATUS: Threatened. Only about 7,000 left in the wild, due to hunting, loss of habitat, and competition with livestock.

---

C C
Paste
C C
Paste
C C

### *Equus asinus*

STATUS: Endangered due to military activity, and competition with domestic livestock for pasture and water.

*Ancestor of today's donkey.*

---

D D
Paste
D D
Paste
D D

### *Equus quagga*

STATUS: Extinct. Hunted to near-extinction. The last quagga died in captivity in 1883.

---

E E
Paste
E E
Paste
E E

### *Equus burchelli*

STATUS: In the early 1960s, millions of Plains zebras roamed the land. Now only 300,000 live in the wild.

---

F F
Paste
F F
Paste
F F

### *Equus ferus przewalskii*

STATUS: Over 1,000 Przewalski's horses are now in zoo captive breeding programs. Some will soon be reintroduced into the wild.

*Ancestor of today's domestic and feral horse.*

---

G G
Paste
G G
Paste
G G

### *Equus hemionus*

STATUS: Endangered. Fewer than 2,000 of each subspecies (onager, kulan, khur, and kiang) live in the wild.

---

H H
Paste
H H
Paste
H H

### *Equus caballus*

STATUS: Generally abundant, but controlled to reduce impact on native wildlife, habitat, and/or livestock.

*Cut along dashed line to remove page from book*

PLAINS ZEBRA

MOUNTAIN ZEBRA

PRZEWALSKI'S HORSE

GREVY'S ZEBRA

AFRICAN WILD ASS

ASIATIC WILD ASS

FERAL (DOMESTIC) HORSE

QUAGGA

HABITAT: Different habitats among locations in North and South America, Australia, France, England, and Japan.

H    H
Paste
H    H
Paste
H    H

Cut along the dashed lines only.

Paste on the shaded letters only.

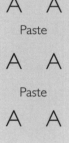

HABITAT: Isolated pockets of mountain habitat in Namibia and South Africa.

A    A
Paste
A    A
Paste
A    A

HABITAT: Southern Africa, prior to extinction.

D    D
Paste
D    D
Paste
D    D

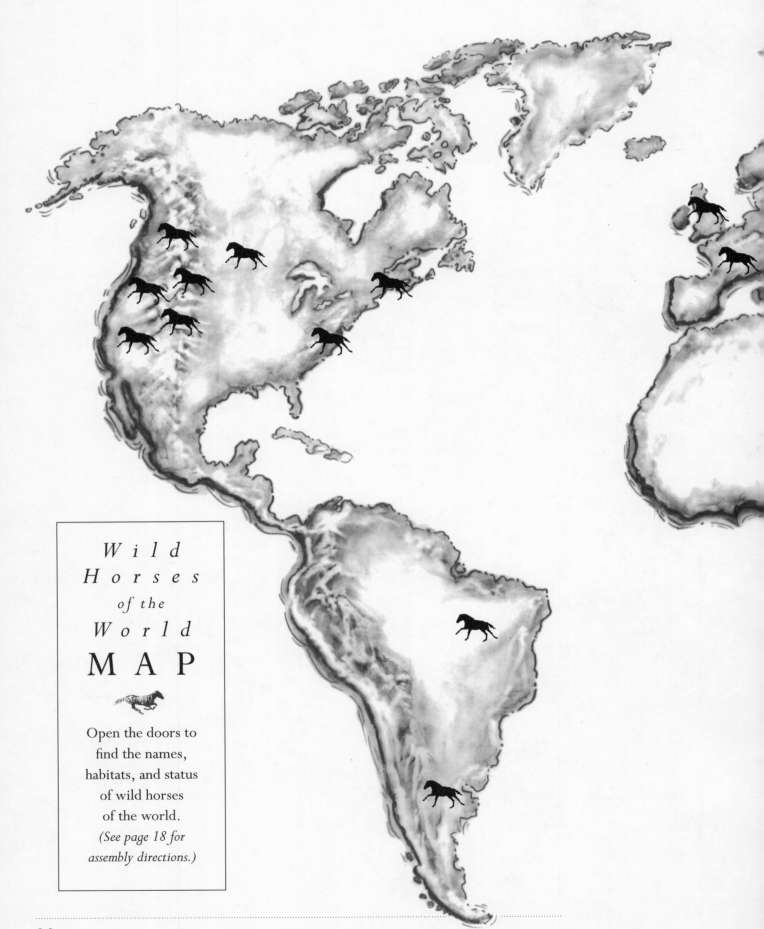

*W i l d*
*H o r s e s*
*o f   t h e*
*W o r l d*
# M A P

Open the doors to
find the names,
habitats, and status
of wild horses
of the world.
*(See page 18 for*
*assembly directions.)*

F F
Paste
F F
Paste
F F

HABITAT: Deserts and semiarid grasslands of southern Mongolia and northern China.

*Wild Horses*
*of*
*North America*
## MAP KEY

*Major North American Wild Horse Herds*

_____

_____

_____

_____

*See page 64 to check your answers.*

G G
Paste
G G
Paste
G G

HABITAT: Lowland deserts of western and central Asia and the Tibetan plateau.

Cut along the dashed lines only.

Paste on the shaded letters only.

C C
Paste
C C
Paste
C C

HABITAT: Rocky areas with scrub vegetation and scarce water in Ethiopia and Somalia.

B B
Paste
B B
Paste
B B

HABITAT: Dry open plains and grass-bush country of northern Kenya and Ethiopia.

E E
Paste
E E
Paste
E E

HABITAT: Open grasslands, savannahs, and grass-bush country of eastern and southern Africa.

# Wild Horses of North America

> *Whoa, Nellie! Here's a map of home!*

> *Oooo—wee!. . . look at that key! Some of them names are as tangled as yer tail.*

Nellie and her cartoon companion have approximately 40,000 real, wild relatives living in the western United States. Another 1,000 or so live on five islands off the Atlantic Coast, and nearly 800 live in Canada.

The wild horses of the American West, or mustangs, do not live in one giant group. They live in smaller groups, often isolated from each other by mountain ranges. Each of these groups is further divided into small family units, or **bands**.

You probably won't see mustangs if you travel across the American West. They live in remote areas, far from people and development. But if you see vast, open spaces of grass and sagebrush, close your eyes and imagine. They might just be there!

## Wild Horses of North America MAP KEY

1. British Columbia
2. Saskatchewan
3. **greOno**
4. Idaho
5. Montana
6. North Dakota
7. **moWingy**
8. California
9. **devaNa**
10. **tUha**
11. Colorado
12. Arizona
13. New Mexico
14. Islands off Maryland, Virginia, North Carolina, and Georgia
15. Nova Scotia

**O B J E C T I V E**

◆ Match the numbers on the map to the key to see in which states or provinces wild horses live.

**Y O U   N E E D**

◆ A pencil

**T O   D O**

◆ Unscramble the bold names to find the areas with the largest wild horse herds. Write your answers in the box on page 24. See page 64 to check your answers.

# Eons of Equids

**E**on means more time than you can measure. **Equid** means horse. In other words, horses have been around forever. Well . . . at least it seems that way! Horses have been roaming the earth for 57 million years!

If you're like most people, the passage of 57 million years is hard to think about. It's so beyond our experience that we can't imagine it. But we can imagine a two-hour movie on videotape.

Let's pretend a film producer has condensed 57 million years of horse history into a two-hour movie. That works out to about 8,000 years of history for every second of videotape! But don't worry—you won't get dizzy watching. Details have been cut out, and the result is a summary of major events in the **evolution** of the horse. Evolution is the change of an animal or a plant over time.

Settle back onto your imaginary couch, grab your make-believe remote, and push "Play."

*Before even the title, little* Hyracotherium, *the first horse, appears on the TV screen. Soon* Orohippus, *another early horse, appears. "They're smaller than dogs!" you exclaim, and keep watching. Generation after generation of horses unfold. You're well into the second hour—the horses' legs are getting longer, their heads bigger—but you still haven't seen it, the one you recognize. The movie is almost over, only 8 minutes (4 million years) left, and finally—there it is!* Equus! *the modern-day horse . . . 112 minutes (53 million years) in the making!*

*But wait, just before the movie ends you see a creature in the background. It looks a little funny, but it is walking on two legs. You're stunned! "What?!" you exclaim. "Humans evolved almost 55 million years after the first horse?"\**

Now you know just how old horses are!

\*Horses and humans evolved on different continents. Horses evolved in North America. Humans, who evolved over 2 million years ago in Africa, migrated into North America only about 15,000 years ago.

# Timeline History of Horses in North America

Horses are old, but they haven't been around forever. The earth is 4.5 billion years old. If the earth's history were reduced to videotapes, you'd have to watch almost 79 two-hour movies before horses evolved. Just think of the popcorn you'd eat!

Before you reach for the popcorn popper, try creating your own summary of horse evolution. Construct an illustrated "History of Horses" timeline.

## OBJECTIVE

◆ Piece together the history of the horse by building a timeline.

## THIS ACTIVITY INCLUDES

◆ "Timeline" descriptions on pages 28, 29, and 30
◆ "Timeline" pictures on page 31
◆ "The Missing Link" pictures and descriptions on page 33

## YOU NEED

◆ Scissors
◆ Paste, glue, or tape

## TO DO FIRST

1. Cut out the pictures from page 31 along the dashed lines.
2. Each picture matches a certain description at the bottom of pages 28–30. Place the pictures in correct order by matching the era names on the back sides of the pictures to the era names above the descriptions. An **era** is a stretch of time in the evolution of an animal or plant.
3. Line up the shaded Xs on the back side of the pictures with the shaded Xs above the description. Paste shaded Xs only. When the paste is dry, lift each picture to read the description underneath.

## THE MISSING LINK

◆ But wait—your timeline isn't complete. Ten thousand years are missing! What happened to horses after they disappeared from North America? How did they get back? Answer these questions by constructing the timeline's missing link. Then bring the horses around the world and back again by adding the link to the timeline.

## TO ADD THE MISSING LINK

1. Cut out the strip of "The Missing Link" descriptions on page 33 along the dashed lines. Cut out the pictures from page 33 along the dashed lines.
2. Match the shaded Xs on the wrong side of the strip of descriptions to the shaded Xs on the edge of page 30. Paste the strip of descriptions to page 30 so they extend off the page to the left with the type facing up.
3. Place the pictures in correct order by matching eras, just as you did earlier.
4. Line up the shaded Xs and paste, as you did earlier. When the paste is dry, lift each picture to read the description underneath. You now have added the Missing Link!

## AFTER ASSEMBLING

◆ Fold "The Missing Link" over page 30 to keep it in your book.

## EOCENE ERA
*(57—34 million years ago)*

*Hyracotherium* lived from
57 to 50 million years ago

## OLIGOCENE ER
*(34—24 million years ago)*

*Mesohippus* lived from
37 to 29 million years ago

The timeline above, and the one you can build below on this page and the next two pages, are similar to the imaginary videotape mentioned on page 26, but with even fewer details. **Timelines** highlight only the big events in history in the order they occurred. They are a good way to sum up long stretches of time.

Sometimes timelines can be misleading, though. For example, by only looking at the timeline pictures and not reading the text, you could assume that horse evolution happened in a straight line—from *Hyracotherium* directly to *Equus.*

Actually the evolutionary path of the horse is more like a family tree with many branches that died out. In the end, the tree looks like it was struck by lightning: nearly dead but not completely . . . one live branch remains—the genus *Equus.*

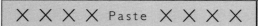

XXXX Paste XXXX  XXXX Paste XXXX  XXXX Paste XXXX

### EOCENE ERA
*(57—34 million years ago)*

Over 50 million years ago, the first horses evolved. They were only a foot tall, the height of little dogs. *Hyracotherium* scampered around, eating leaves in the tropical forests of western North America. They had three toes on the front feet and four on the back. The middle toes each had developed into a tiny pointed hoof.

### OLIGOCENE ERA
*(34—24 million years ago)*

Time passed and horses kept changing. *Mesohippus* and other ancestors of today's horses grew taller. They lost their fourth hind toe and their middle hooves got bigger. Their molars were short and still suited for eating leaves in the forests and along streams where they lived.

### MIOCENE ERA
*(24—5 million years ago)*

The world's climate became cooler and drier. Grasslands were as common as forests. Many kinds of three-toed horses roamed the woodlands and wide-open spaces. *Merychippus* may have been one of the first grazing horses. They were able to run more quickly than earlier horses.

**P L E I S T O C E N E   E R A**
*(2 million –10,000 years ago )*

**M I O C E N E   E R A**
*(24–5 million years ago)*

**P L I O C E N E   E R A**
*(5–2 million years ago)*

**H O L O C E N E   E R A**
*(Modern Era, 10,000 years ago to present)*

*Merychippus* lived from 21 to 12 million years ago

*Pliohippus* lived from 15 to 8 million years ago

*Equus,* the present-day horse, first appeared 4 million years ago

*(Humans didn't appear until about 3.5–4 million years ago)*

*Equus,* present-day horse

# H O R S E   F A M I L Y   T R E E

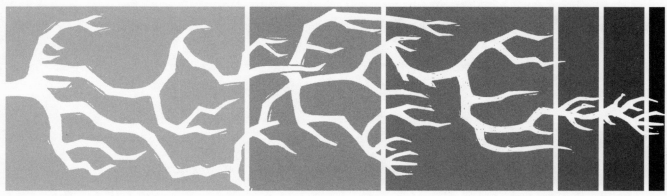

*Equus,* present-day horse

In the past 57 million years, the horse family tree has had many branches. Nearly 250 types of horses have come and gone since little *Hyracotherium* ran through the forest!

✕ ✕ ✕ ✕ Paste ✕ ✕ ✕ ✕   ✕ ✕ ✕ ✕ Paste ✕ ✕ ✕ ✕   ✕ ✕ ✕ ✕ Paste ✕ ✕ ✕ ✕

**P L I O C E N E   E R A**
*(5–2 million years ago)*

Many kinds of horses evolved from *Merychippus,* including *Pliohippus,* the first one-hoofed horse. And then, about 4 million years ago, true horses arose! They were members of the genus *Equus,* the same group today's horses represent. They had long legs for running fast, and large, strong teeth for eating gritty, fibrous grasses.

**P L E I S T O C E N E   E R A**
*(2 million–10,000 years ago)*

*Equus* migrated from North America into Asia across the Bering Land Bridge. From there, they migrated into Africa and Europe 2 million years ago. Other horses stayed and flourished in North and South America. They even survived the Ice Age!

**L A T E   P L E I S T O C E N E   E R A**
*(approximately 10,000 years ago)*

*Equus* in North and South America completely disappeared 10,000 years ago. Why? Theories range from overhunting by prehistoric Indians to major climate change. Many other large mammals died out after the last Ice Age when habitats changed dramatically. The mystery is still unsolved.

### INDIANS AND HORSES

The arrival of domestic horses changed the lives of American Indians forever. Instead of making long, slow journeys on foot, they rode and packed their gear on fleet-footed horses. They traded more with other tribes, hunted buffalo with greater ease, and expanded their hunting territories to cover vast stretches of prairie.

Tribes centered their activities around their horses, sometimes moving only to seek better pasture. Horses became symbols of wealth and power. Tribes without horses were handicapped during warfare. Those with horses painted, decorated, and blessed them before battle. It's no surprise that horse images fill the folklore, mythology, songs, and art of American Indians.

*My horse has a hoof like striped agate;*
*His fetlock is like a fine eagle-plume;*
*His legs are like quick lightning.*
*My horse's body is like an eagle-plumed arrow;*
*My horse has a tail like a trailing black cloud.*

—Navajo song

*Dakota Indian drawings:*
*hoofprints (above), horse and teepee.*

---

#### 1540s

Nearly 10,000 years after horses disappeared from North America they returned with Spanish explorers better known as conquistadores. Cortez, Coronado, and other conquistadores traveled north through Mexico into what is now the southwestern United States.

#### 1540 TO 1770

The first North Americans to meet the conquistadores were afraid of the white men's "giant dogs." In time, they overcame their fear and acquired many for themselves. From 1680 to 1770, horses spread northward among the Indians. Plains Indians became widely known for their exceptional riding skills.

#### 1770 TO PRESENT

Today's wild herds are a melting pot of horse breeds. Some show the markings of Spanish Andalusians. Others resemble the sturdy pony-like horses of the Indians. Still others are descendants of European breeds that were brought west by settlers from the East Coast. Last are the recent arrivals—work and pleasure horses from today's ranches.

| Hyracotherium | Mesohippus | Merychippus |

| Pliohippus | Equus | *Equus* disappears from North and South America |

| Horses return | Indians and horses | Wild horses today |

*M I O C E N E  E R A*
*(24–5 million years ago)*

*O L I G O C E N E  E R A*
*(34–24 million years ago)*

*E O C E N E  E R A*
*(57–34 million years ago)*

*L ATE  P L E I S T O C E N E  E R A*
*(approximately 10,000 years ago)*

*P L E I S T O C E N E  E R A*
*(2 million–10,000 years ago)*

*P L I O C E N E  E R A*
*(5–2 million years ago)*

*1 7 7 0  T O  P R E S E N T*

*1 5 4 0  T O  1 7 7 0*

*1 5 4 0 s*

See page 27 for directions to add "The Missing Link" to your "Timeline History of Horses in North America."

## The Missing Link

X X X X  Paste  X X X X  X X X X  Paste  X X X X  X X X X  Paste  X X X X

### RECENT HISTORY
*(500 years ago to present)*

Just over 500 years ago, the Spanish brought the prized Andalusians to the New World aboard Spanish ships. They were suspended in slings draped between beams below deck so they would not fall. Only the strongest horses survived the two- to four-month journey. Once on land they became breeding stock, supplying horses for the Spanish conquest of new lands.

### RECENT HISTORY
*(5,000–500 years ago)*

Humans began riding horses about 5,000 years ago. A thousand years ago, Spanish horsemen started breeding fast, sleek desert horses with big, strong European war horses. The result was the Spanish Andalusian, a combination of the two.

### LATE PLEISTOCENE ERA
*(approximately 10,000 years ago)*

*Equus* had migrated throughout Asia, Africa, and Europe. By the late Pleistocene, isolation had resulted in the evolution of today's distinct horse groups: zebras of Africa; wild asses of northern Africa and Asia, and the true horses, such as the Przewalski's horse of western Asia.

## Horses are brought to the Americas

## Horses are domesticated

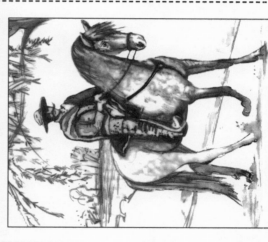

## Equus species evolve

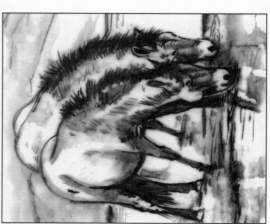

Paste  Paste  Paste

**RECENT HISTORY**
*(500 years ago to present)*

Paste

**RECENT HISTORY**
*(5,000–500 years ago)*

Paste

**LATE PLEISTOCENE ERA**
*(approximately 10,000 years ago)*

Paste

# The tale of Talk-Not

The tale of Talk-Not is a **fable**, a make-believe story that describes something real. It's not about wild horses, but don't dismay. This tale can teach you a lot about how horses, humans, and all other species change over time.

The Kingdom of Talk-Not was a tiny place where people never talked. Not talking wasn't simply a choice; it was natural. No one talked, or nearly no one. Once, by nature's whim, a chatty child was born. It was sheltered by its mother, and miraculously grew up to have children of its own. But, only a few of them survived. One peep out of their sweet mouths, and they were gone—licked by the flames of a dragon's deadly breath. You see, the dragons of Talk-Not were not fond of talk.

Suddenly, the dragons all died. No one knows why; they just did. Not-talking was no longer necessary. But that didn't matter. No one talked because no one could—except the few chatty children who survived the dragon's breath.

Then the serpents slithered into the kingdom. Stepping on a serpent meant certain death—or near certain. Only under one circumstance was a Talk-Notter spared the serpent's deadly squeeze—only if he or she could tell the serpent a story. Poor people of Talk-Not. They couldn't tell a story if their lives depended on it. And unfortunately, their lives did.

Only the chatty children survived the serpents. And since the dragons had all died, more of the chatty children were around. They grew up stepping on serpents, but the serpents didn't mind. They were forever charmed by the children's endless stories. These children grew up and had children of their own, who grew up and had more chatty children.

In time the Kingdom of Talk-Not was filled with people who talked *A LOT*.

# Natural Selection at Work

Like all good fables, *The Tale of Talk-Not* holds some truth. It describes **natural selection**, a process of change that every species experiences in its evolution. This process works on wild horses and humans alike.

Before natural selection can work there must be **variation**, or different traits, within a group of animals. For example, humans have blue, green, and brown eyes. Or, as in the Kingdom of Talk-Not, some people couldn't talk and others talked a lot.

Variation results from **mutations**, sudden changes that occurred long ago, or even recently in traits. Contrary to popular belief, some mutations can be very helpful, as in the case of the chatty child.

If a mutation helps an animal survive and reproduce, the new trait will be passed on to the next generation. This process is exactly what happened to the chatty children. Being able to talk and tell stories helped them survive. They grew up and had chatty children of their own.

Natural selection is always at work, but the results are easiest to see when the environment changes. Natural selection weeds out animals not suited for the new environment. When the dragons died and the story-loving serpents moved in, the people who couldn't talk were doomed. If not for the mutation that produced the chatty child, everyone in Talk-Not would have died. The people of the kingdom would have gone extinct.

So, the moral of the story is . . . species must mutate to survive!

Mutations are partly why horses still live in the world today. They have mutated many times in their long history. The most helpful mutations brought about **adaptations**, traits that helped them survive in their changing environment. As the tropical forests changed to dry grasslands, natural selection favored horses with traits such as long legs, single hooves, and big, strong teeth.

# Designer Horses

*L*ike designer clothes, designer horses are tailored by humans. Instead of brand names, designer horses have breed names . . . such as Arabian and Thoroughbred.

**THOROUGHBRED**
*beauty and speed*

The process of designing horses is better known as horse breeding. Horse breeding is similar to natural selection. The main difference is that humans, not the environment, select the traits that survive. Each pairing of male and female horse involves careful, educated decisions.

For example, when the Nez Perce Indians wanted to create a strong yet beautiful working horse, they paired their sturdiest mounts with their prettiest spotted horses. Only the foals with the best of both traits—strength and beauty—were bred. The result was a horse that has become one of America's most popular breeds—the Appaloosa. (The name comes from the Palouse River of Washington and Idaho in the Nez Perce homeland.)

**QUARTERHORSE**
*intelligence and swiftness*

**APPALOOSA**
*strength and beauty*

# Nature Selects

On the next page is a silhouette of a Przewalski's horse. This species lives in the mountains and deserts of central Asia. Although the Przewalski's horse is the likely ancestor of the domestic horse, it evolved with little or no influence from humans. Only nature selected its traits for survival.

Put the puzzle together. Watch a truly wild horse take shape before your eyes!

## OBJECTIVE

◆ Put a puzzle together to learn the traits of a truly wild horse.

## THIS ACTIVITY INCLUDES

◆ The Przewalski's horse silhouette on page 39
◆ The puzzle pieces on page 41

## YOU NEED

◆ Scissors
◆ Paste or glue

## TO DO

1. Read the traits of the horse on page 39. Cut out the corresponding body parts from page 41. Put the puzzle together on top of the silhouette on page 39.

2. When finished, glue the pieces in place.

## TRAITS OF THE TRULY WILD

Although similar in form, the Przewalski's and domestic horses do differ. Many of these differences are due to domestication and breeding.

| PRZEWALSKI'S HORSE | DOMESTIC HORSE |
| --- | --- |
| Erect mane | Flowing mane |
| No **forelock** (mane on forehead) | Forelock |
| Top of tail is bare | Full tail |
| Mane and tail shed all at once | Mane and tail not shed at once |
| 66 **chromosomes** (strands of genes) | 64 chromosomes |
| One coat color | Many coat colors |
| Shorter, pony-like | Taller |
| Larger brain | Smaller brain |
| Stronger hooves | Weaker hooves |

The wild horses of the American West descended from domestic horses. They share many of the same traits. However, the longer mustangs remain in the wild, the more time nature has to select the traits best suited for their survival. Some biologists say that mustangs are gradually becoming shorter and smarter, and have stronger hooves than domestic horses.

# PRZEWALSKI'S HORSE

**Eyes**—placed high on head to help see over grass when grazing, and for seeing behind and in front at the same time

**Ears**—large and mobile, good for detecting predators

**Fur**—thick and as long as 3 inches (8 cm) in the winter

**Body**—large enough to provide adequate space for big lungs and vital organs, but small enough to be quick and agile

**Coat color**—light brown coloration provides **camouflage** (protective coloration)

**Neck**—long, helpful for grazing and while searching for predators

**Head**—elongated shape for housing 30 big, grass-grinding molars, large brain for aiding survival in the wild

**Tail**—long and coarse, good for swatting flies

**Leg muscles**—bunched at the tops to provide the greatest movement with the least effort

**Legs**—long and light-boned, good for outrunning predators

**Hooves**—strong, able to withstand running on hard, rocky ground without splitting

# Grinding Machine

A horse skull is a chewing and grinding machine! Each of the 36 teeth and 2 jawbones is a well-designed machine part. The jawbones move the teeth up and down, and side to side. Front teeth called the **incisors** grab and rip the grass. The large, flat **premolars** and **molars** grind the grass until it's soft and ready to swallow.

Incisors and **canines** do more than chew. They are also used for grooming, threat displays, and biting. The four canines may have evolved as specialized weapons. With a firm bite to the leg, a horse's canines can sever a challenger's **tendon**, the band of tissue connecting muscle to bone.

## OBJECTIVE
◆ Build a horse skull to learn about its teeth and jaw movements.

## THIS ACTIVITY INCLUDES
◆ The skull, jaw, and spring strips on the next page

## YOU NEED
◆ Scissors
◆ Paste or glue

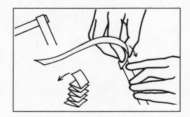

How to fold strips into springs

## TO DO
1. Cut out the skull, jaw, and spring strips from page 41 along the dashed lines. Cut two slots in the skull along the dashed lines.

2. Make two springs. Place one spring strip over another at right angles. Paste the ends together. Fold the strips over each other at right angles until you reach the ends. Paste the ends together. Repeat with the other two strips. See picture at left.

3. Paste one end of each spring to an ✕ on the jaw of the diagram below. Paste the other ends of the springs to the ✕s on the back of the cutout jaw.

4. Fold the tabs on the cutout skull under along the solid lines. Paste the tabs to the diagram, matching the shaded letters. Weave the bone of the lower jaw through the slots of the skull.

Operate the grinding machine by moving the lower jaw up and down, side to side, and all around.

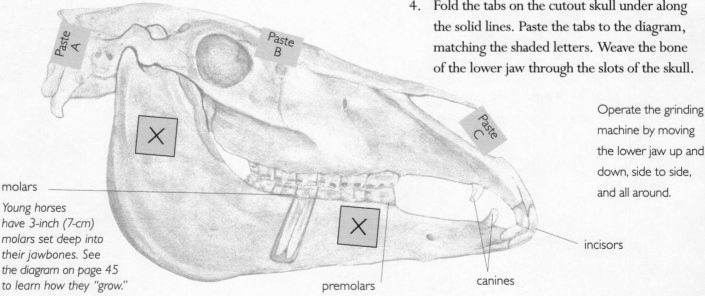

molars

*Young horses have 3-inch (7-cm) molars set deep into their jawbones. See the diagram on page 45 to learn how they "grow."*

Paste A

Paste B

Paste C

premolars

canines

incisors

# GRINDING MACHINE

See page 40 for directions.

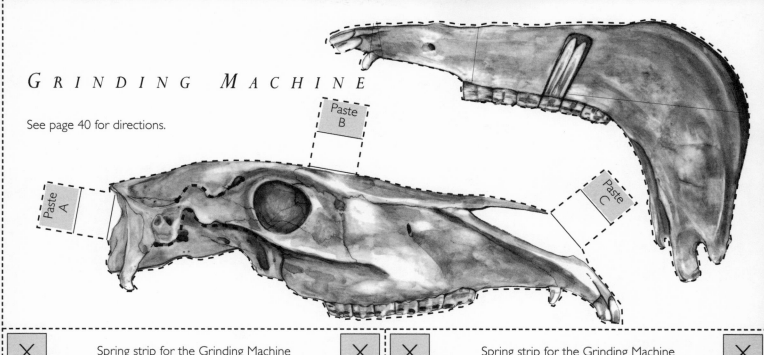

Paste A

Paste B

Paste C

| | Spring strip for the Grinding Machine | | | Spring strip for the Grinding Machine | |
|---|---|---|---|---|---|
| X | | X | X | | X |
| X | Spring strip for the Grinding Machine | X | X | Spring strip for the Grinding Machine | X |

# PRZEWALSKI'S HORSE PUZZLE

See page 38 for directions.

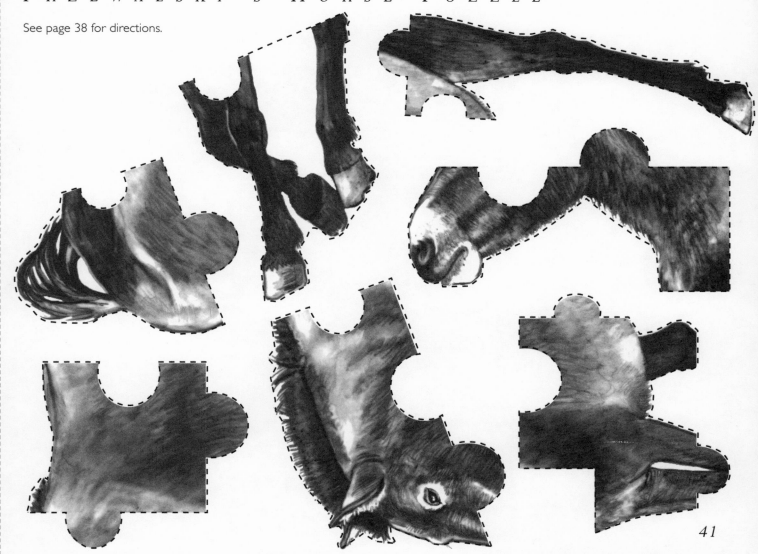

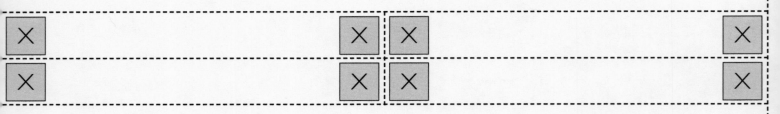

# Island Horses

Far from mustang country is a long sliver of sand dunes and saltmarshes called Assateague Island. Located off the coast of Virginia and Maryland, Assateague is home to about 350 wild horses. A spirited foal named Misty brought fame to the island horses. She was the main character in *Misty of Chincoteague,* an award-winning book by Marguerite Henry.

Assateague horses are the size of ponies. Poor nutrition probably stunts their growth. They nibble prickly briars and poison ivy, but their main foods are saltmarsh grasses. The salty grass makes them thirsty. Island horses drink two times more freshwater than most horses!

Historians believe that horses have lived on Assateague Island for over 300 years. Most think that farmers brought them to the island to avoid putting up fences or paying mainland taxes. In time, the horses were forgotten and they began to behave like wild horses.

Not just any horse can live on Assateague Island. When a disease killed many island horses, wild mustangs were brought from California to increase the herd. Most of the mustangs died, apparently unable to survive on the saltmarsh diet. Many of the first Assateague horses may have died, too. But in time these hardy little horses adapted to their island home.

It's possible to adopt an island horse. Each July the Chincoteague Volunteer Fire Company rounds them up, swims them across a channel to Chincoteague Island, and auctions some of the foals. The popular event is called Pony Penning Day. For over 100 years it has attracted large crowds of horse lovers like you!

4 inches (10 cm)

**Ponies** are horses that are less than 14 hands tall at their shoulders. A **hand** equals 4 inches (10 cm). Although Assateague horses are usually shorter than 13 hands, their foals often grow to horse size if fed nutritious food. True ponies do not grow taller than 14 hands, even if fed the best food!

Are Assateague horses bigger than you? Trace this hand to measure yourself or your friends.

# *Wild Horse Food Facts*

ild horses don't dine on buckets of grain or bales of sweet hay. Instead they eat an assorted selection of wild plants—anything from high-fiber bunchgrasses to prickly sprigs of juniper.

Wild horses choose the most nutritious and best-tasting plants available, but are not finicky when faced with starvation. They're survivors. They'll switch to shrubs when snow buries their preferred grasses. They'll seek greener pastures during a drought. Below are some of the common wild horse foods of the dry desert West.

In the spring and summer, wild horses eat nutritious bunchgrasses such as

INDIAN
RICEGRASS
*(Oryzopsis hymenoides)*

BLUEBUNCH
WHEATGRASS
*(Agropyron spicatum)*

WESTERN
WHEATGRASS
*(Agropyron smithii)*

When snow becomes too deep to push aside and uncover the grass, horses eat the tastier, more nutritious shrubs such as

WINTERFAT
*(Ceratoides lanata)*

BITTERBRUSH
*(Purshia tridentata)*

FOURWING
SALTBUSH
*(Atriplex canescens)*

If snows are especially deep or food is scarce, wild horses survive on foods such as

ROCKY MOUNTAIN JUNIPER
*(Juniperus scopulorum)*

QUAKING ASPEN BARK
*(Populus tremuloides)*

OLD HORSE DUNG

*By eating horse dung, horses benefit from nutrients that weren't used the first time through.*

## HOW MUCH DOES A HORSE EAT?

The average horse consumes about 25 pounds (11 kg) of plants in a day! For comparison, a large dog eats about 25 pounds of meaty dogfood in a month. In general, plant-eaters, such as horses, eat more than meat-eaters, such as dogs. Pound for pound, plants have less nutritional value than meat.

Consuming 25 pounds of plants takes a lot of time. Horses spend an average of 12 hours per day grazing!

With all the chewing and grinding, how do horse teeth hold up? Horse molars are covered with an especially thick layer of **enamel**, a protective coating that resists wear—perfect for eating fibrous, gritty grasses. Molars also grow throughout a horse's life, or at least they *appear* to grow. A young horse has 3-inch (7-cm) molars set deep in the jawbone. As the molars wear down with use, the jawbone fills in at the base of the tooth sockets, nudging the molars into the mouth.

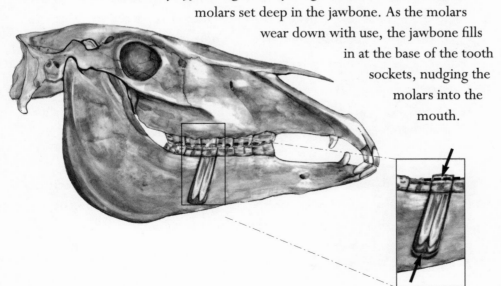

# Horse of a Different Color

When people say "That's a horse of a different color," they're usually not talking about horses at all. This colorful expression describes anything that is recognizable in form, but unusual in some other way. For example, a person dressed in a tiger-stripe suit would be a horse of a different color.

On the next page are true horses of a different color—wild horses recognizable in form, but different in coat color, pattern, or texture. Because these traits are rare among horses, they are admired and sometimes sought after by wild horse enthusiasts.

## OBJECTIVE

◆ Learn to identify coat colors and unusual wild horse traits.

## YOU NEED

◆ Crayons or colored pencils

## TO DO

1. Read the descriptions below. Search the herd and find six horses with these unusual patterns and textures.
2. Refer to the Color Key to color the horses according to their traits.

### CURLY COATS

Some wild horses have curly fur and wavy manes and tails. They are descendants of Russian Bashkirs, large ponies brought to the American West in the 1800s. The thick, curly coats are an adaptation to the cold and snow of the Baskhir's native Russia. *Color this trait **sorrel** or **bay***.

### MEDICINE HATS

Pintos with large dark patches on their chests and over their ears are called Medicine Hats. To the Plains Indians the markings symbolized a protective shield and headpiece. Medicine Hats were considered sacred and were the prized mounts of many Indian warriors. *Color this trait **pinto***.

### LEG STRIPES

Dark stripes around the legs are a trait of horses that evolved long ago. Where wild horse herds are isolated and less influenced by modern breeds, horses with leg stripes are occasionally born. *Color this trait **dun***.

### DORSAL STRIPES

A dark stripe down the center of a horse's back is called a **dorsal stripe**. Przewalski's horses have dorsal stripes, as did most primitive horse species. Striping is usually associated with primitive coat coloration: yellow-brown, grey-brown, or blue-grey. Together they provide excellent camouflage. *Color this trait **dun** or **grey***.

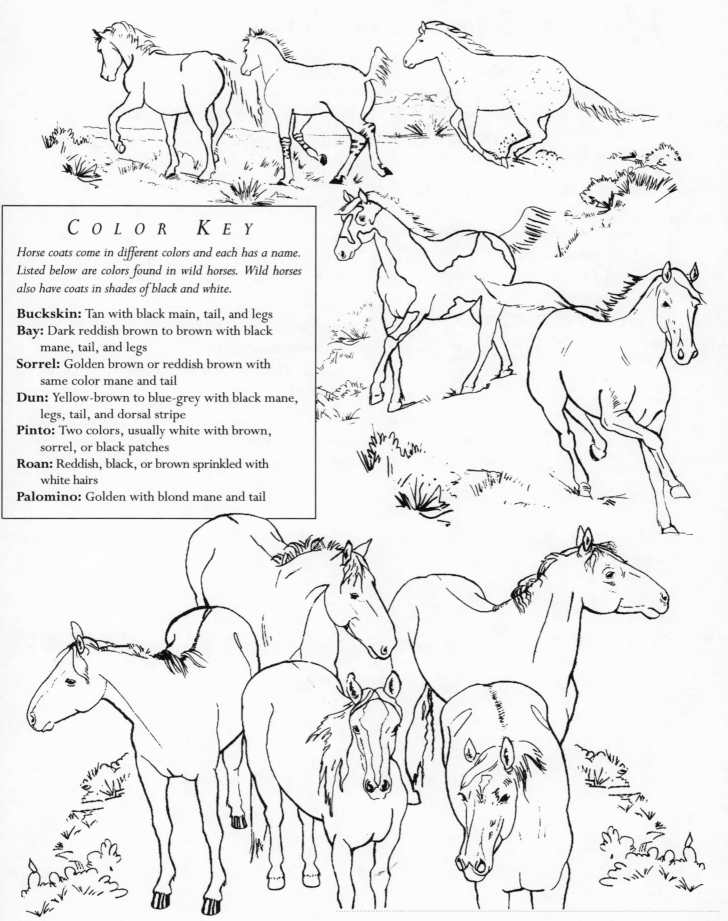

## COLOR KEY

*Horse coats come in different colors and each has a name. Listed below are colors found in wild horses. Wild horses also have coats in shades of black and white.*

**Buckskin:** Tan with black main, tail, and legs

**Bay:** Dark reddish brown to brown with black mane, tail, and legs

**Sorrel:** Golden brown or reddish brown with same color mane and tail

**Dun:** Yellow-brown to blue-grey with black mane, legs, tail, and dorsal stripe

**Pinto:** Two colors, usually white with brown, sorrel, or black patches

**Roan:** Reddish, black, or brown sprinkled with white hairs

**Palomino:** Golden with blond mane and tail

# Harems, Bands, and Herds

Technical terms are sometimes confusing. Take harems, bands, and herds, for instance. What's the big difference . . . they're all a bunch of horses, right?

*The horse family glossary:*

**Stallion**—a male horse that is old enough to mate

**Mare**—a female horse that is old enough to mate

**Foal**—an offspring of a stallion and a mare

**Yearling**—a foal between one and two years old

**Bachelor**—a young male that has left the harem

Well, sort of right, but sort of wrong. Harems, bands, and herds are all groupings of horses, but the makeup of each is different.

A **harem**, or band, is the family group. It is made up of mares, foals, and yearlings. The harem is guarded by a stallion. He mates with all the mares and is the father of his harem's foals.

When young male horses, or **bachelors**, are about two years old, the stallion forces them to leave the harem. They join other males in **bachelor bands.** Members of a bachelor band tend to come and go. Eventually most find mates, start a harem, and leave, but some never do.

A **herd** refers to all the bands living in a particular area. You rarely see herds together at once unless food is scarce. Also, if horses are frightened, harems and bachelor bands will sometimes join together in a great, running herd.

*Far off on a mesa a string of mustangs was running . . . their tails streamed o*

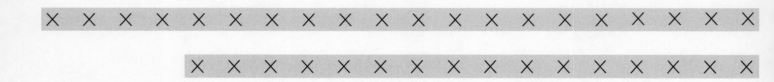

*Subdominant mare and foal*

*Dominant mare and foal*

## WHY DO HORSES BAND TOGETHER?

Wild horses have a better chance of seeing and escaping predators if they live together. Living in a band may also make it easier for horses to find scarce food and water.

Each member of a band knows its place in the band's **hierarchy**, or ranking of power. Although it's better to be ranked higher than lower, being in a band and having a low rank is safer than being alone.

## DO STALLIONS DEFEND TERRITORIES?

Most wild stallions do not defend specific **territories**, or land areas. They defend harems instead. Stallions keep their harems together, and drive away other males. By doing so, each stallion makes sure that he is the father of his harem's foals.

Stallions of Grevy's zebras and the Asian and African wild asses are different. They defend territories, not harems.

*ind and their manes lifted like licks of flame.*
—Marguerite Henry

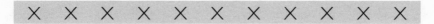

*Stallion*

*Subdominant mare*

# Pop-up Wild Horse Herd

You might be surprised to learn that the stallion isn't the only harem boss. The **dominant**, or most powerful, mare is an equally important leader.

When a harem is in danger, the dominant mare decides the direction and the course of the fleeing band. With ear and eye signals, and occasional kicks and bites, she keeps her harem in line. If the stallion dies, the harem usually stays together, led by the dominant mare.

The stallion's main job is defending his harem. He stands guard, and if necessary, chases off intruders. In a running band the stallion is usually at the rear. There he can place himself between the harem and danger, and nip and push to drive the horses faster.

## OBJECTIVE
◆ Learn about herd hierarchy by building a pop-up wild horse herd.

## THIS ACTIVITY INCLUDES
◆ Pop-up wild horse cutouts and scenery on page 51
◆ Site for running horse harem on pages 48 and 49
◆ Descriptions of harem hierarchy on pages 48 and 49

## YOU NEED
◆ Scissors
◆ Paste, tape, or glue

## TO DO
1. Cut out the horses and scenery from page 51 along the dashed lines.
2. Fold the shaded strips under along the solid lines.
3. Paste the scenery down on pages 48 and 49 by matching the ✕s on the shaded strips to the ✕s on the pages. Paste the horses down on pages 48 and 49 by matching the hoofprints on the shaded strips to the hoofprints on the pages.
4. Read the names in front of each horse to learn its position in the herd hierarchy.

# P O P - U P   C U T O U T S

See page 50 for directions.

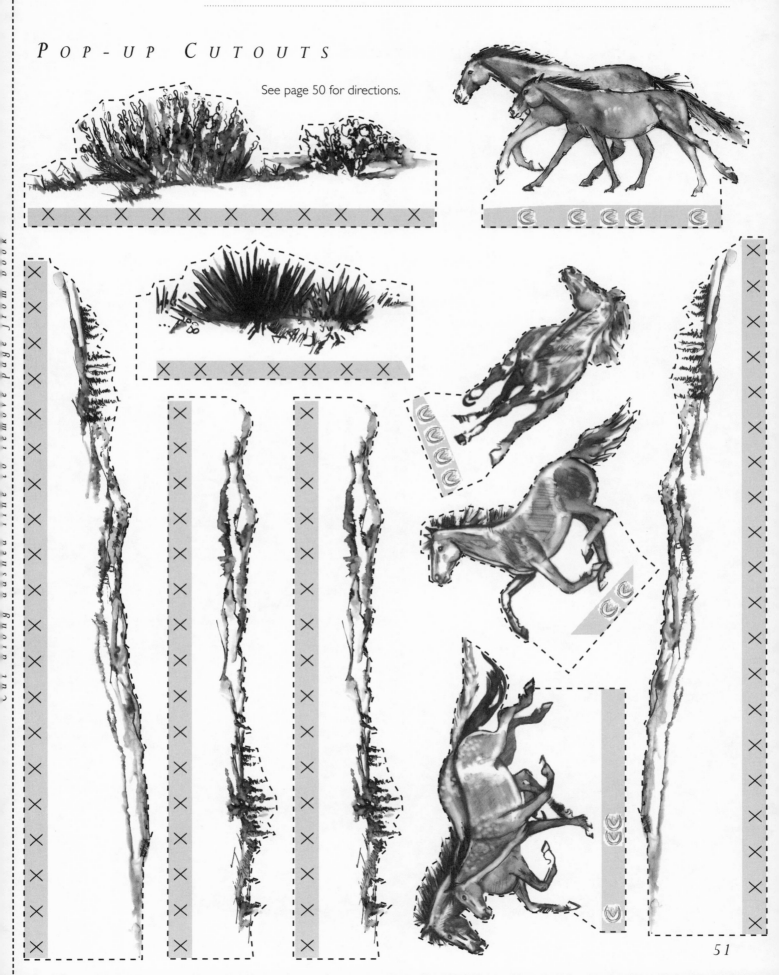

# GET THE MESSAGE BOOKLET  See page 55 for directions.

-7-
"Hmmm . . . that smells interesting!"

-10-
"Move it! Move it! Get going! Hurry up!"

-9-
"I'm afraid!"

-4-
"Get out of here, NOW!"

This guide translates horse body language so you can see what the horses are "saying" on page 55. Write the page number of your answer in the box next to each horse. Check your answers on page 64.

-1-

-2-
"I'm feeling great, let's play!"

# HOLD ONTO YOUR HAREM!
# BOARD GAME PLAYING PIECES  See page 56 for directions.

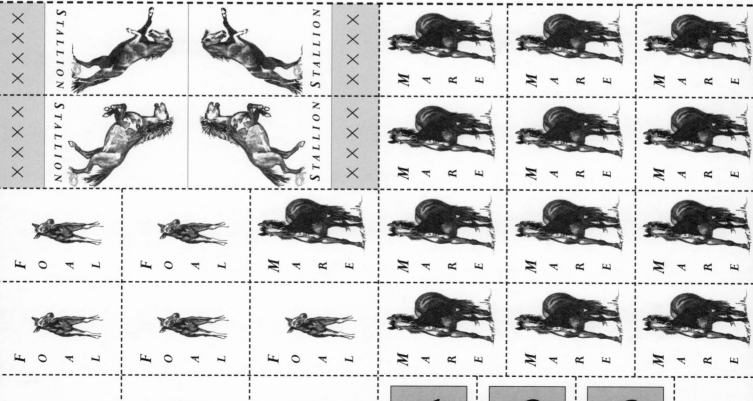

STALLION  STALLION
STALLION  STALLION

MARE  MARE  MARE
MARE  MARE  MARE
FOAL  FOAL  MARE  MARE  MARE  MARE
FOAL  FOAL  FOAL  MARE  MARE  MARE
FOAL  FOAL  FOAL

1  2  3

53

"I like you, you're
my friend."

-8-

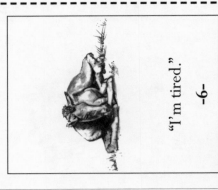

*H O R S E
S E N S E*

*A Guide to Horse Body
Language for Humans*

"I'm tired."

-6-

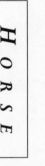

"Wanna fight?"

-3-

"This doesn't look good,
I'd better investigate."

-5-

# Body Language

Cut out and place pages 1 and 10 face up.

Fold pages at bottom up. Fold top down. Pages 5 and 6 face up.

Fold in half like a book, with cover face up.

Trim the top and bottom only. Staple through the center.

Psychologists tell us that the key to getting along with others is good communication. Wild horses have known that for years—millions of years! They are social animals and their survival depends on living in bands. Communicating makes living together easier.

To communicate, horses have developed a language all their own. Horse language is more than neighing and squealing. It also involves sniffing each other's scents and reading each other's body language.

Horses communicate mostly through body language. The way a horse holds its head or moves its body sends messages to other horses. Two important ways of communicating are the position of a horse's ears and the "look" in its eyes.

Horse body language isn't too different from our own (except for ear positions!). For instance, horses stomp their feet when they are frustrated, and they open their eyes wide when they are frightened or surprised.

After creating your very own "Guide to Horse Body Language" for humans, see if you can tell what the horses on this page are "saying." Some messages may be easier to translate than others.

### OBJECTIVE
◆ To understand horse body language.

### THIS ACTIVITY INCLUDES
◆ The "Horse Sense" booklet on page 53
◆ The diagram and illustration on this page

### YOU NEED
◆ Scissors
◆ A pencil
◆ A stapler

### TO DO
1. Cut out the booklet from page 53 along the dashed lines.
2. Fold, trim, and staple the booklet as shown in the diagram above.
3. Read page 1 of the booklet for instructions on how to translate the horse body language illustrated on this page.

# Hold onto Your Harem!

The first thing a stallion needs to know is "Hold onto your harem!" A stallion **herds**, or gathers and protects, his harem to ensure that he has as many foals of his own as possible—and that they survive. It's a big job! He stands guard, chases off intruders, and drives away predators. Sometimes he threatens and even fights with rival stallions.

Herding is a stallion's instinct. Every day, stallions herd their harems as they move toward water, away from danger, or into a stand of trees. But two times each year, stallions herd their harems on a longer journey—from summer to winter range and back again. These migrations are as predictable as the birds'. But instead of traveling north and south, horses move up and down mountainsides.

Snow falls early in the high country, usually in autumn. When snow covers the grass, the horses move down to the valleys for winter. Eventually snow will fall there, too, but the valleys stay warmer and the low slopes have trees for shelter.

By late spring or summer, the horses are ready to move back up the mountain. Plants in the valley are wilting in the heat, but in the mountains snow is melting, and green grasses are growing.

In this activity, you are a stallion. It's your role to herd your harem as quickly and safely as possible from summer to winter range. The snows are coming, so don't delay. And watch out for predators and horse thieves along the way!

## OBJECTIVE
◆ Be the first stallion to enter the winter range with a harem (excluding you, the stallion) of at least four.

## THE GAME INCLUDES
◆ The game board on pages 58 and 59
◆ The game pieces and tokens on page 51

## YOU NEED
◆ Crayons or colored pencils
◆ Scissors
◆ A cup or small paper bag

## BEFORE PLAYING
◆ Color the scenery on the game board on pages 58 and 59.
◆ Cut out the game pieces and tokens from page 53. Fold and paste the stallion playing pieces as shown in the diagram on page 57.
◆ Read the directions on page 57.

Cut out stallion playing pieces. Fold shaded tabs to inside.

Fold in half with stallions facing out.

Paste shaded tabs together to make stand.

Finished stallion playing piece.

## DIRECTIONS TO PLAY
*(for two players)*

1. Each player begins with one stallion (the playing piece), three mares, and one foal. Place the extra mares and foals in two separate piles next to the game board.

2. Put numbered tokens into a sack or cup, and shake. Each player picks a number. The player with the highest number goes first.

3. The first player picks another number, and advances that many spaces on the board. Players alternate turns.

4. Follow the directions on the space where you land. Each space describes a realistic experience and interaction between wild horses.

5. If you land on a space that tells you to take another turn or move to another space, follow the directions on that space too. Jumping the ravine counts as one space.

6. You may move around the board in any direction. You may choose a shorter, more dangerous route or a longer, safer route.

7. To gain mares or foals, pick from the piles and add to your harem. If there are no more mares, pick a foal instead, or vice versa. If you lose mares or foals, take them from your harem and put them in the pile(s).

8. The winner is the first stallion to enter the winter range with a harem of four or more, made up of any number of mares and foals. If you lose some of your harem on the way, you will have to reverse your course to gather the number you need. Good luck surviving the cold, snowy winter!

## MIGRATION MANIA!

If you've mastered the migration routes and want more fun and challenge, consider adding the following rules.

1. If you land on the same space as your opponent, steal one of his or her mares. Then follow the directions on that space.

2. To win the game, you must get to the finish in the exact number of spaces. If you choose a number greater than the number of spaces to the finish, you must stay on your space and wait for your next turn.

See page 57 for directions.

*Summer Range*

**START**

Pregnant mare stops to give birth. **Gain one foal.**

Young mare joins another herd. **Lose one mare.**

Windy day—feel frisky. **Jump over ravine.**

**Jump over ravine.**

Encounter wandering mare and foal. **Gain one mare and one foal.**

To escape biting flies, detour herd to windy ridgeline. **Move back one space.**

Bureau of Land Management wild horse roundup. **Lose two mares.**

Mare escapes from roundup. **Gain one mare.**

Encounter another stallion who steals a mare. **Lose one mare.**

Especially wet year, food nutritious and abundant. **Take another turn.**

Mare gives birth to foal while harem sleeps. **Gain one foal.**

Foal ambushed by mountain lion at water hole. **Lose one foal.**

Another herd comes to water hole. Steal mare before moving on. **Gain one mare.**

Sickly mare revived by visit to water hole. **Take another turn.**

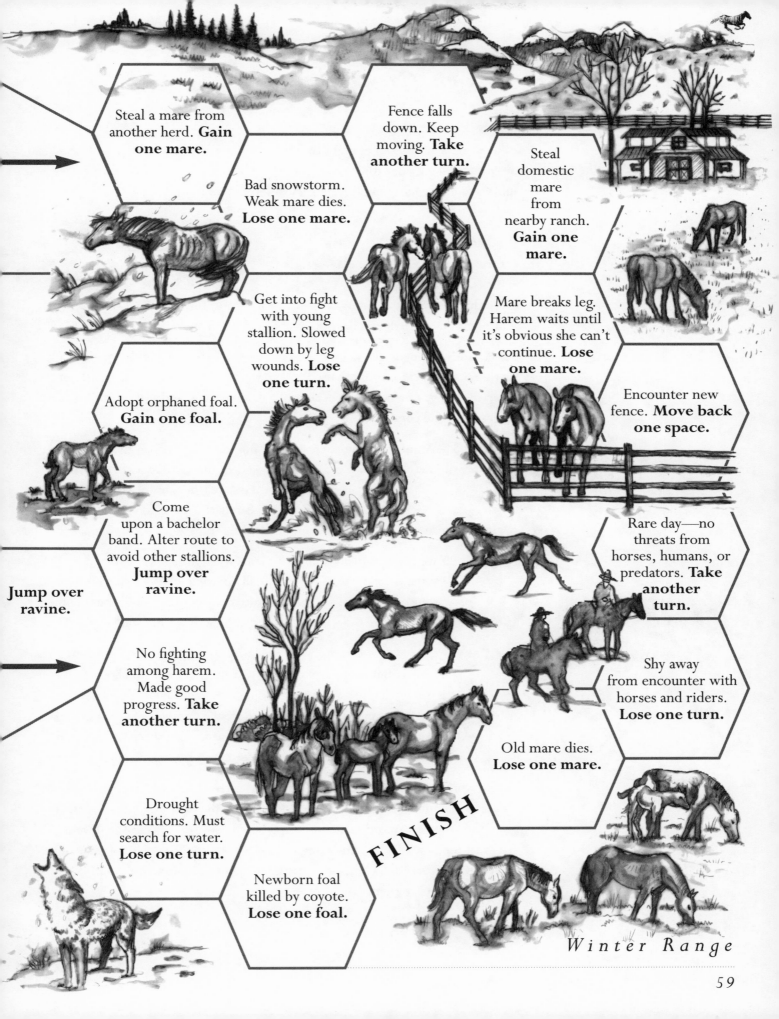

Steal a mare from another herd. **Gain one mare.**

Fence falls down. Keep moving. **Take another turn.**

Steal domestic mare from nearby ranch. **Gain one mare.**

Bad snowstorm. Weak mare dies. **Lose one mare.**

Get into fight with young stallion. Slowed down by leg wounds. **Lose one turn.**

Mare breaks leg. Harem waits until it's obvious she can't continue. **Lose one mare.**

Adopt orphaned foal. **Gain one foal.**

Encounter new fence. **Move back one space.**

Come upon a bachelor band. Alter route to avoid other stallions. **Jump over ravine.**

Rare day—no threats from horses, humans, or predators. **Take another turn.**

**Jump over ravine.**

No fighting among harem. Made good progress. **Take another turn.**

Shy away from encounter with horses and riders. **Lose one turn.**

Old mare dies. **Lose one mare.**

Drought conditions. Must search for water. **Lose one turn.**

**FINISH**

Newborn foal killed by coyote. **Lose one foal.**

*Winter Range*

# The Wild Horse Controversy

**H**ave you ever said something that within minutes had your friends in a heated debate? If so, your topic was a controversial one. **Controversies** are subjects about which people have very different opinions.

Wild horses are controversial animals. Most people agree that they are interesting creatures, even beautiful. But not everyone believes they should be running free on U.S. public lands.

Public lands belong to the people. People pay taxes to maintain them, and they have a say in how the lands are used. Some want these lands used for cattle or sheep ranching, others for the benefit of native wildlife, and still others for wild horses, or some combination of the above.

All of these people have valid points. Wild horses, livestock, and native wildlife compete for many of the same foods. When more horses are allowed to live on public lands, fewer cows, sheep, and native wild animals can. Similarly, more cows and sheep mean fewer wild horses and less wildlife.

If we allow as many animals to live on public lands as everyone wants, the habitat would eventually be ruined. Too many mouths would devour the vegetation. Too many hooves would trample the plants, erode the streambanks, and pack down the soil.

The wild horse controversy, like all controversies, is difficult to solve. But people are trying. Many ranchers and wild horse supporters are concerned about rangeland habitat. They support the government's decision to reduce the numbers of livestock and wild horses living there. Wildlife managers are also protecting the habitat by reducing the numbers of wildlife in certain areas.

People working for the Bureau of Land Management, many wild horse supporters, and kind-hearted adopters have made the Adopt-A-Horse or Burro Program a success. Additionally, scientists have been working hard to develop a drug that temporarily prevents some mares from having foals. Use of the drug will limit growth of wild horse numbers, but will not replace the Adopt-A-Horse or Burro Program.

Controversies can be troubling, or even upsetting, if people become angry at each other. But controversies can also lead to progress. When people are free to voice their opinions, even unpopular ones, there is more information on which to base decisions.

The decisions about wild horses probably won't please everyone, but they may satisfy many. And more important, they may protect the habitat for animals today and in the future.

## OPINIONS SURROUNDING THE WILD HORSE

Over the past four decades the controversy surrounding the mustang has ranged from mild disagreements to angry arguments. Below are some opinions about wild horses. They are not actual quotes. What do *you* think?

*These beautiful creatures have been tormented for years. It's about time wild horses were given more room and better habitat.*

*Controlling the size of wild horse herds makes sense if it reduces starvation and protects the land. But I insist on humane treatment of each horse during the roundups.*

*Those "broomtails" are a bunch of no-good freeloaders—eating grass that doesn't belong to them. Wild horses ought to be removed from the range to make more room for cattle!*

*Wild horses are scapegoats for some people's problems. Western rangelands are too dry to support cattle, and instead of admitting it, we blame helpless horses!*

*Why spend all this time and money on wild horses? If they're wild animals, let nature take its course— starvation, disease, and all!*

*Wild horses aren't wild—they're just a bunch of stray pets or ranch runaways. I say let's remove all these range robbers and give real wildlife a chance!*

# Wild Horse Annie

In a time when wild horses were viewed as enemies of cattle ranching, a woman called "Wild Horse Annie" fought to protect them. She wasn't the rootin', tootin' cowgirl her nickname implies. To the contrary, Annie was a small, polio-stricken secretary who was—believe it or not—allergic to horses!

Annie's real name was Velma Bronn Johnston. She was born in Nevada in 1912. As a girl and young woman she never thought of herself as a leader or wild horse expert. But one day in 1951, that began to change. Mrs. Johnston encountered a truck filled with battered, bleeding wild horses. Shocked and angered by what she saw, and remembering what she'd read about cruel treatment of mustangs, she vowed on the spot to protect them.

Velma became a strong and determined leader on behalf of wild horses . . . so strong that angry opponents gave her the name "Wild Horse Annie" in hopes of discrediting her efforts. But as Annie often did, she turned a negative into a positive, and embraced her new name. She made it the symbol of her wild horse campaign!

In the late 1950s, Annie turned to children for help. At her request, they flooded the offices of members of Congress with letters—so many letters that they couldn't be ignored! The children expressed their anger and concern about the treatment of mustangs, and Congress listened. In 1959 Congress passed the Save the Mustangs Bill, the first national law for the protection of wild horses.

The 1959 bill had many benefits, but it was difficult to enforce. Mustangers continued to treat wild horses inhumanely as they rounded them up and sold them off for pet food. Annie and her supporters pushed forth a stronger bill, the 1971 Wild Free-Roaming Horse and Burro Act. Contained within the act are words that must have been music to Annie's ears:

> Congress finds and declares that wild free-roaming horses and burros are living symbols of the historic and pioneer spirit of the West; . . . that [they] shall be protected from capture, branding, harassment . . .

People who knew Annie say her remarkable accomplishments were due to her organizational skills, her knowledge of the facts, her love of horses, and her compassion for all people, even the ranchers and mustangers who opposed her work.

Wild Horse Annie died in 1977. Annie's undying spirit lives on today in the free-roaming horses of the American West, and in citizens, wherever they live, who fight to make a difference.

# Glossary

**adaptation** (ad ap TAY shuhn)—a trait that helps an animal or a plant survive in its environment

**bachelor** (BATCH uh luhr)—a single, typically young male horse that does not have a harem

**bachelor band** (BATCH uh luhr BAND)—a group of single male horses

**band** (BAND)—a small group of horses

**bay** (BAY)—reddish brown coat with black mane, tail, and legs

**buckskin** (BUHK skin)—tan coat with black mane, tail, and legs

**camouflage** (KAM uh flahzh)—coloration that helps animals hide

**canines** (KAY nynz)—sharp, pointed teeth used for grooming, threat displays, and biting; rarely found in females of many horse species

**chromosomes** (KROH muh sohmz)—strands containing an individual's genes

**conquistador** (kohn KEES tuh dohr)—Spanish leader and explorer in the conquest of the Americas

**controversy** (KAHN truh vuhr see)—a subject about which people have very different opinions

**domesticated** (duh MEHS tih kayt id)—tamed or brought into use by humans

**dominant** (DAHM uh nuhnt)—most powerful

**dorsal stripe** (DOHR suhl STRYP)—a dark stripe down the center of the back

**dun** (DUHN)—yellow-brown to blue-grey coat with dark mane, tail, and legs

**enamel** (ihn AM uhl)—the hard protective coating on teeth

**eon** (EE ahn)—a long period of time that is immeasurable or indefinite in length

**equid** (EHK wid)—a member of the horse family

**Equus** (EHK wuhs)—the genus into which scientists group all living horses, zebras, and asses

**era** (IR uh)—a period of time in the development of an animal, plant, or thing

**evolution** (ev uh LOO shun)—the change of an animal or plant over a long period of time

**fable** (FAY buhl)—a make-believe story intended to teach something true

**feral** (FEHR uhl)—that which lives in the wild but was once domesticated

**foal** (FOHL)—a horse less than one year old; the offspring of a stallion and a mare

**forelock** (FOHR lahk)—mane growing on the forehead

**genus** (JEE nuhs)—a scientific grouping of closely related species

**habitat** (HAB uh tat)—the place or type of place where an animal or a plant normally lives

**hand** (HAND)—a unit of measurement used for the height of horses; one hand equals 4 inches (10 cm)

**harem** (HAR uhm)—a family group made up of several mares, their foals, and yearlings, all guarded by a stallion

**herd** (HURD)—(noun) a group made up of all the harems and bachelor bands in a particular area; (verb) to gather and keep together

**hierarchy** (hy uh RAHR kee)—the ranking of power of a horse band's members

**Hyracotherium** (hy rak uh THEER ee uhm)—the tiny first horse that lived 57 to 50 million years ago

**incisors** (ihn SY zuhrz)—front teeth used for grabbing and cutting

**mare** (MAIR)—a female horse capable of mating

**Merychippus** (mair ih KIP uhs)—a three-toed horse ancestor that lived 21 to 12 million years ago; may have been one of the first grazing horses

**Mesohippus** (mez oh HIP uhs)—a forest-dwelling horse ancestor that lived 37 to 29 million years ago

**molars** (MOH luhrz)—large, flat back teeth used for grinding

**mustang** (MUHS tang)—a small, hardy, western horse whose ancestors were horses brought to North America by Spanish explorers

**mutation** (myoo TAY shuhn)—a sudden change in a trait

**natural selection** (NACH uh ruhl suh LEK shuhn)—the process that causes the survival and continuation of individuals best suited to their environment and the removal of those that are not

**Orohippus** (or oh HIP uhs)—a horse ancestor that lived in the Eocene era

## GLOSSARY, CONTINUED

**palomino** (pal uh MEE noh)—golden coat with blond mane and tail

**pinto** (PIN toh)—mostly white coat with patches of brown, sorrel, or black

**Pliohippus** (plee oh HIP uhs)—the first horse ancestor that had only one hoof on each foot; lived 15 to 8 million years ago

**pony** (POH nee)—a horse less than 14 hands tall at the shoulder

**premolars** (pree MOH luhrz)—large, flat teeth in front of the molars that are also used for grinding

**roan** (ROHN)—reddish, black, or brown coat sprinkled with white

**sorrel** (SAWR uhl)—golden brown or light brown coat with same color mane and tail

**species** (SPEE sheez)—a scientific grouping of closely related individuals with common traits; a type or a kind of plant or animal

**stallion** (STAL yuhn)—a male horse capable of mating

**tendon** (TEHN duhn)—a tough band of tissue connecting muscle to bone

**territory** (TEHR uh tohr ee)—an area occupied and defended by an animal

**timeline** (TYM lyn)—a linear graph showing when major events occurred

**variation** (ver ee AY shuhn)—different traits or characteristics within an animal or plant population

**yearling** (YIHR lihng)—a horse that is between one and two years old

## Bibliography

Berger, Joel. 1986. *Wild Horses of the Great Basin.* University of Chicago Press, Chicago.

Clark, LaVerne Harrell. 1966. *They Sang for Horses: The Impact of the Horse on Navajo and Apache Folklore.* University of Arizona Press, Tucson.

Clutton-Brock, Juliet. 1992. *Horse Power.* Harvard University Press, Cambridge.

Edwards, Elwyn H. 1993. *Horses: The Visual Guide to Over 100 Horse Breeds from Around the World.* Dorling Kindersley, New York.*

Jauck, Andrea, and Larry Points. 1993. *Assateague: Island of the Wild Ponies.* Macmillan Publishing Co., New York.*

Kieper, Ronald R. 1985. *The Assateague Ponies.* Tidewater Publishers, Centreville, Maryland.

Kirkpatrick, Jay F. 1994. *Into the Wind: Wild Horses of North America.* Northword Press, Minocqua, Wisconsin.

Ryden, Hope. 1990. *America's Last Wild Horses.* Lyons and Burford, New York.

Symanski, Richard. 1985. *Wild Horses and Sacred Cows.* Northland Press, Flagstaff, Arizona.

Thomas, Heather S. 1979. *The Wild Horse Controversy.* A. S. Barnes and Co., Inc., Cranbury, New Jersey.

Vavra, Robert. 1979. *Such Is the Real Nature of Horses.* William Morrow and Company, Inc., New York.*

Waring, George H. 1983. *Horse Behavior.* Noyes Publications, Park Ridge, New Jersey.

Wexo, John Bonnett. 1986. *Zoobooks: Wild Horses.* Wildlife Education, Ltd., San Diego.*

* These books are of interest to younger readers.

## ANSWER KEY

### ADOPT-A-HORSE PROGRAM, page 16

〚ᚾᚱᛏᛌᛚᛇ〛 91 243801—Colorado

〚ᚠ ᛥᚢ∣∣ᚱᛍ〛 92 557120—Nevada

〚ᚠ ᚢᚢᛃᛍᛕᛍ〛 94 776090—Utah

### WILD HORSES OF NORTH AMERICA
page 25

**greOno**—Oregon
**moWingy**—Wyoming
**devaNa**—Nevada
**tUha**—Utah

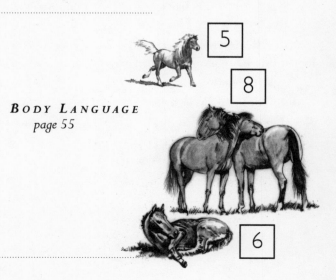

**BODY LANGUAGE**
page 55

5

8

6